FOR JOAKIM

First edition 2006

Library of Congress Cataloging-in-Publication Data

Drescher, Henrik.

Hubert the Pudge : a vegetarian tale / by Henrik Drescher —1st ed

p. cm

Summary: As one of many pudges awaiting their trip to the meat factory at the Pudge Processing Farm, little Hubert the Pudge escapes to the jungle, where the animals show him all the good foods he can eat and, as a result, he becomes the first pudge to achieve full size since ancient times.

ISBN-10 0-7636-1992-2

ISBN-13 978-0-7636-1992-3

[Imaginary creatures—Fiction. 2. Animals—Fiction. 3. Jungles—Fiction. 4. Vegetarianism—Fiction.] I. Title

PZ.D78383Hu 2006

[E]—dc22 2005058211

2 4 6 8 10 9 7 5 3 1

Printed in Singapore

This book was typeset in URW Egyptienne.

The illustrations were done in colored pencil and ink.

Candlewick Press

2067 Massachusetts Avenue

Cambridge, Massachusetts 02140

visit us at www.candlewick.com

HUBERT THE PUDGE
A Vegetarian Tale

HENRIK DRESCHER

CANDLEWICK PRESS
CAMBRIDGE, MASSACHUSETTS

ubert the Pudge grew up on Farmer
Jake's Pudge Processing Farm. Actually,
to say that he "grew up" would be wrong.

1 month

Because pudges never got a chance
to fully grow up. While they were still
young, they were trucked off to the meat
factory, where they were processed into
TV dinners, microwave sausage links,
and other greasy food products.

Every part of the pudge was used.
Even the squeal, which was canned
and installed in car alarms and foghorns.

2 months

3 months

4 months

5 months

6 Months

7 Months

8 months

One day each year, while the barn was being cleaned, the pudges were allowed to play in the yard, eating fresh clover, daffodils, and cobwebs (pudges adore cobwebs).

They dreamed of life on the other side of the tall fence, a place where no pudge's knuckle had ever trod.

Out in the grass, beside the fence, Hubert
was chomping on juicy spring cobwebs, when
suddenly a small hole in the fence caught his eye.

Quicker than you could say "fried pudge chops,"
Hubert squeezed through the hole and dashed
for freedom!

Swiftly he ran though the meadow.

Thistles tickled his chubby belly;

the wind whistled in his ears.

His short legs propelled him with great

speed, and before nightfall he reached

the great green jungle.

Hubert spent his first day frolicking in the forest, feeding on luscious grass, exotic orchids, and skunk cabbage.

When night fell, Hubert
huddled under a banana
tree, trying to sleep, but
the freaky night sounds
kept him awake:

HOOT!

HOWL!

HISS!

The jungle was alive!

In the morning he introduced himself to the owners of the creepy night sounds, who weren't that creepy at all. They showed him the fun and yummy foods of the jungle.

Soon Hubert was taller than a boa is long and wider than a hippo.

The bigger he grew, the more he ate . . .

The more he ate, the bigger he grew.

Until one fine day Hubert became the first full-grown pudge since ancient times.

He was GiANt!

He was HUMONGOUS!

He was SUPERCHUNKY-NORMOUS!!

He was big enough to give pudgy-back rides to elephants!

His days were spent chomping coconut

trees, without a care in the world. . . .

Well, almost without a care.

Sometimes at night, memories

of his doomed friends at the farm

came flooding back to Hubert.

One particularly bad night, he

was overcome with sadness

and cried a river of tears.

The next morning Hubert could stand it no longer. With a BLAST! from his trunk, he summoned the other animals to help him rescue his friends.

They tromped out of the jungle.

As they crossed the savanna, this time it was the palm trees that tickled his belly. All night they marched. By morning they arrived at Farmer Jake's Pudge Processing Farm.

Hubert gently peeled the roof off the pudge barn.

Everyone was jubilant. They scurried into the dawn.

Then Hubert greeted Farmer Jake, who was
gorging himself on deep-fried pudge knuckles.
When he saw Hubert, he nearly choked.
After making him promise to stop picking
on pudges and find something better to do
with his life, Hubert let Farmer Jake down.

From that day on, everything changed at the farm.

The pudge processing was put to an end.

All pudges were allowed to roam freely, growing
bigger and bigger to their natural size, as Hubert had.

As for Farmer Jake, he stopped eating pudge and started to work out at the gym, where he met Heidi, his trainer.

They fell in love and were married.

Together they started Jake and Heidi's Tofu Hot Dogs Company. They hired pudges to turn the giant tofu mill. (They were paid in cobwebs.)

Their tofu hot dogs were a rip-roaring success because they were healthful and tasted much better than the real thing.

Everyone lived happily and healthily ever after . . .

especially the pudges.